MARVEL STUDIOS

THOR

HEROES & VILLAINS

Adapted by Elizabeth Rudnick
Based on the screenplay by Ashley Edward Miller & Zack Stentz and Don Payne
Story by J. Michael Straczynski and Mark Protosevich

NEW YORK

Published by Marvel Press, an imprint of Disney Publishing Worldwide. No part of this book may be reproduced or transmitted in any form or by any means, electronic or mechanical, including photocopying, recording, or by any information storage and retrieval system, without written permission from the publisher. For information address Marvel Press, 114 Fifth Avenue, New York, New York 10011-5690.

Printed in the United States of America

First Edition

1 3 5 7 9 10 8 6 4 2

J689-1817-1-11046

ISBN 978-1-4231-4635-3

THIS IS ASGARD

For centuries, it has been one of the most powerful of the Nine Realms. The men and women who call it home have superhuman strength, live for thousands of years, and are extremely loyal to Asgard's present ruler. . . .

INSIDE the magnificent palace, which towers over the city, live Asgard's royalty—King Odin Allfather; his queen, Frigga; and their sons, Thor and Loki.

This is a guide to the citizens of Asgard, its enemies, and the connected realm of Midgard, better known to mortals as planet Earth.

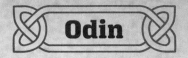

Odin

Aliases: Allfather, King of Asgard

Relatives: Father, Bor (deceased); mother, Bestia (deceased); brothers, Ve and Vili (both deceased); wife, Frigga; sons, Thor and Loki

Abilities/Attributes: The mightiest of the Asgardians. Odin wields a massive power source called the Odinforce, which allows him to control energy and the elements.

Weapons: Gungnir, a mighty spear filled with the Odinforce.

Animals: Eight-legged steed named Sleipnir who can run on land and air.

Story: The ruler of Asgard, Odin wants to pass the throne on to his eldest son, Thor. But he worries his son is not ready. When he is forced to banish Thor

To possess and use the Odinforce is very draining. At various times over the course of his reign, the king has to enter Odinsleep. This restores his powers.

to Midgard, Odin becomes distraught and falls into a deep Odinsleep.

Frigga

Name: Frigga, Queen of Asgard

Relatives: Husband, Odin; sons, Thor and Loki

Abilities/Attributes: Beauty, Asgardian strength, and great patience.

Story: As Odin's wife, Frigga has been his constant companion and voice of reason for centuries. Loyal and true, she is also a loving mother to Thor and Loki. While she tries not to, she favors her youngest, Loki, who is often in the shadow of Thor. After Thor is banished and the king goes into Odinsleep, she relies heavily on Loki, for better or worse.

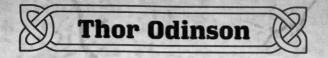

Thor Odinson

Aliases: Warrior of Asgard, Son of Odin, the mighty Thor

Relatives: Father, Odin; mother, Frigga; brother, Loki

Companions: The Warriors Three, Lady Sif

Abilities/Attributes: Thor possesses physical powers superior to those of normal Asgardians. He has an extended lifespan and superhuman strength. (He can lift up to several hundred tons.)

Weapons: Made of uru metal, the mighty hammer Mjolnir lets Thor control lightning, rain, and thunder. Spinning the hammer allows him to fly.

Gear: Thor's helmet is quite distinct. The eagle wings on either side represent his nobility. He usually wears a long red cape and dons ancient Asgardian armor plating.

Story: Eager to take the throne, Thor is quick to act and slower to think. When he leads an attack on the Frost Giants of Jotunheim that threatens a truce between the two realms, Odin is furious. Banished to Midgard by his father, Thor's powers are stripped. He will have to prove he is worthy of the throne and his father's trust before he is allowed back into Asgard.

Loki

Aliases: The Trickster, Master of Magic

Relatives: Father, Odin; mother, Frigga; brother, Thor

Companions: Sticks to himself, but is closest to Thor

Abilities/Attributes: Superhuman strength, increased life span. Regarded as one of the most powerful sorcerers in all of Asgard. He can make himself appear to be somewhere he is not, shape-shift, and teleport. He is often the voice of reason to Thor's impulsiveness and is usually relied on to talk his older brother out of sticky situations.

Gear: Like his brother, Loki also has a helmet that he wears for ceremonial purposes. His features two long horns that curl at the ends. He also wears a green cape.

Story: As Odin's younger son, Loki has always known the throne of Asgard will never belong to him. He has, however, tried his best to be a good brother to Thor and a son Odin could be proud of. When Thor travels to Jotunheim, it is Loki who sends a message to their father in order to prevent an all-out war. Still, he cannot stop Odin from banishing Thor. When the king falls into Odinsleep soon after, Loki takes the throne.

The Warriors Three

Name(s): The Warriors Three are Volstagg the Voluminous, Fandral the Dashing, and Hogun the Grim

Companions: Thor, Loki, Lady Sif

Attributes: Known on Asgard as the strongest and bravest of men, they rarely leave Thor's side. Volstagg is large, even for an Asgardian, and he enjoys everything to excess. His belly is one of his greatest weapons, but he is also very gifted with an ax. Fandral thinks quite highly of himself, and his ego often gets him in trouble

VOLSTAGG
THE VOLUMINOUS

FANDRAL THE
DASHING

HOGUN THE GRIM

with both warriors and ladies. He is incredibly good with an ax and fights as hard as he plays. The most serious of the three, Hogun is a deadly warrior and wields a mace with grim accuracy. He doesn't speak often, but when he does, it is important to listen.

Story: As loyal friends to Thor, the Warriors Three agree to travel with him on his ill-fated trip to Jotunheim. While there, Fandral is injured, and all three are almost killed by Frost Giants. It is only Odin's arrival that saves them. When Thor is sent to Earth and Loki becomes King, the Three, plus Sif, begin to suspect everything is not as it seems. . . .

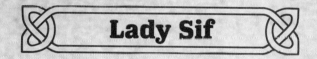

Lady Sif

Companions: Thor, Loki, The Warriors Three

Attributes: The fourth member of Thor's entourage, Sif is the fiercest of Asgard's female warriors. She carries a shield and a carved sword and is often the first to leap into battle. But Sif is also a voice of reason, and she often tries to consul Thor—even when he doesn't want to hear it.

Heimdall

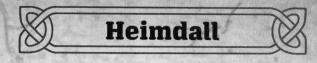

GUARDIAN OF THE RAINBOW BRIDGE

Occupation: Controls the Bifrost and Rainbow Bridge; grants Asgardians the ability to enter and leave Asgard through various portals. The Bifrost Control is the device that starts the Bifrost.

Abilities/Attributes: Superhuman strength and super senses that enable him to hear and see across realms. Heimdall's eyes are a very striking orange color.

Weapons: His sword can be inserted into the control device to open the Bifrost—but it is also a mighty weapon.

Story: Tasked with guarding the Rainbow Bridge, an attack on Asgard occurs on Heimdall's watch. To try to figure out who is behind it, Heimdall allows Thor, Loki, the Warriors Three, and Lady Sif to travel to Jotunheim . . . with disastrous results.

Frost Giants, Jotuns

Realm: Jotunheim

Attributes: Extremely large (bigger even than Asgardians) and strong. Able to withstand extremely cold temperatures.

Weapons: The Frost Giants have the ability to mold ice into various weapons using their skin and body structures. Some Frost Giants have large heads that they can use as rams while others have long arms that can form into swords of solid ice.

Story: After Odin took the Casket of Ancient Winters from Jotunheim, the realm began to collapse. Now it is a shadow of its former self, and the Frost Giants who live there are eager to seek revenge. Laufey, king of the Frost Giants, will stop at nothing to once again control the Casket of Ancient Winters, which will return Jotunheim to the power it once enjoyed.

The Destroyer

Relatives: None

Companions: None

Purpose: To destroy. The Destroyer is Odin's fiercest weapon. When deactivated, it looks like a hollow—yet scary—statue. However, when called upon to protect something, the Destroyer fills with Odinforce and is virtually indestructible.

Weapons: The Destroyer's head is used to direct Odinforce directly at the enemy. The visor slides back to allow the energy to escape. The Destroyer is an enchanted suit of armor forged by Odin; its body is unbreakable. The black armor contains rows upon rows of small spikes, so on the rare occasion enemies get past the Destroyer's Odinforce, they still have to deal with its spearlike edges. The Destroyer has no soul and no life.

Story: Thought by many to be a myth, the Destroyer is tasked with guarding the vault, which holds Asgard's most dangerous relics, including the Casket of Ancient Winters.

Jane Foster

Realm: Midgard, or Earth

Companions: Erik Selvig and Darcy Lewis

Occupation: Astrophysicist

Abilities/Attributes: Smarter than the average human, determined, and kindhearted.

Gear: Jane's Pinzgauer, which serves as a research vehicle, helps her to view and record the occurrences happening over the Puente Antiguo skies.

Story: While in her science lab doing research on anomalies in space, Jane witnesses the Bifrost open on Earth. Moments later she accidentally hits a now-mortal Thor with her Pinzgauer and sets in motion a series of events that change the warrior's life. As Thor struggles to figure out what it means to be human, he turns to Jane for advice and comfort. But is there any chance for love between an Asgardian warrior and a human scientist?

Both jaded scientist **Dr. Erik Selvig** and wided-eyed student **Darcy Lewis** are with Jane when she first encounters Thor. While Darcy is eager to help the handsome man, Selvig believes that Jane should leave well enough alone. However, it is Selvig who discovers the connection between Thor and Norse mythology.

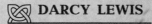 ERIK SELVIG

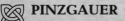 PINZGAUER

DARCY LEWIS

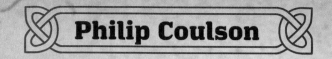

Occupation: S.H.I.E.L.D. agent.

Weapons: As a member of S.H.I.E.L.D., Coulson has access to advanced technology and sophisticated weapons—he even mistakes the Destroyer for one of those weapons.

Story: When S.H.I.E.L.D. becomes aware that Thor and his mystical hammer, Mjolnir, have landed in the New Mexico desert, they send Agent Coulson to investigate. Upon meeting Thor, Coulson suspects the mighty warrior might be a great asset to the top secret Avengers Initiative . . . but will Thor agree?

S.H.I.E.L.D. stands for Strategic Homeland Intervention Enforcement and Logistics Division. Led by Director **Nick Fury,** S.H.I.E.L.D. has agents stationed all over the world.

THESE are the heroes and villains of Asgard and Earth. Known and unknown to each other, they will change each other's lives and the future of their realms forever with the help of the mighty Thor.